HOW TO SURVIVE

SCHOOL DISASTERS

PUFFIN

PUFFIN BOOKS

UK | USA | Canada | Ireland | Australia
India | New Zealand | South Africa

Puffin Books is part of the Penguin Random House group of companies
whose addresses can be found at global.penguinrandomhouse.com.

www.puffin.co.uk

Penguin
Random House
UK

First published 2016
Published in this edition 2017

001

Printed in Italy

A CIP catalogue record for this book is available from the British Library

ISBN: 978-0-241-32968-9

MIX
Paper from
responsible sources
FSC® C018179

Penguin Random House is committed to a
sustainable future for our business, our readers
and our planet. This book is made from Forest
Stewardship Council® certified paper.

HOW TO SURVIVE
SCHOOL DISASTERS

Endless homework, class elections, cheap
toilet paper – Greg Heffley knows exactly
how tough school can be. Find out what
happens when Greg has to solve his homework
problems, find a missing dictionary and help
his best friend Rowley run for student council.
Will it all end in disaster?

**Look out for lots of fun
Wimpy Kid activities in this book!**

HOMEWORK TROUBLES AND MISSING DICTIONARIES

from

THE LAST STRAW

<u>Friday</u>

My new thing is that I take a nap every day after school.

In fact, I LIVE for my naps. Sleeping after school is the only way I can really recharge my batteries, and on most days the second I get home I'm in bed.

I'm actually kind of becoming an expert at sleeping. Once I'm out, I can sleep through just about anything.

The only person I know who's better at sleeping than me is my brother RODRICK, and here's the reason I say that. A couple of weeks ago, Mom had to order Rodrick a new bed because he'd worn his out. So the furniture guys came to take his old mattress and box spring away.

When they came, Rodrick was in the middle of his after-school nap. So they took his bed away, and he just slept on the floor, right in the middle of his empty bed frame.

The thing I'm worried about is that Dad is going to ban our after-school naps. I'm starting to get the feeling he's sick of waking the two of us up for dinner every night.

Tuesday

Well, I hate to admit this, but I think my naps are starting to have an effect on my grades.

See, I used to do my homework when I got home from school, and then I watched TV at night.

Lately I've been trying to do my homework WHILE I watch TV, and sometimes that doesn't work out too good.

I had this four-page Biology paper due today, but last night I kind of got caught up in this show I was watching. So I had to try to write the whole thing in the computer lab during recess today.

I didn't have a lot of time to do any research, so I played with the margins and the font size to stretch what I had to four pages. But I'm pretty sure Ms Nolan is gonna call me on it.

CHIMPS

A four-page paper by

GREG HEFFLEY

1

This is a chimpanzee, or "chimp" for short.

Chimps are the subject of the paper you're holding in your hand right now.

2

Chimps are supposed to be smart, but I'm not so sure that's true.

3

Well, it looks like I'm out of paper, so I guess this is

THE END.

4

Can you help Greg redo his homework by drawing a chimpanzee in the space below?

Here are some fun facts about chimps to wow your friends at school.

🐵 They eat fruit, plants, insects and meat.

🐵 They can live for over sixty years.

🐵 They are our closest living relatives.

Yesterday I actually got a "zero" on a quiz in Geography. But, in my defence, it was really hard to study for the quiz and watch football at the same time.

To be honest with you, I don't think teachers should be making us memorize all this stuff to begin with, because in the future everyone is going to have a personal robot that tells you whatever you need to know.

Speaking of teachers, today Mrs Craig was in a really bad mood. That's because the big dictionary that usually sits on her desk was missing.

I'm sure someone just borrowed it and forgot to put it back, but the word Mrs Craig kept using was "stole".

Mrs Craig said that if the dictionary wasn't returned to her desk before the end of the period she was keeping everyone inside for recess.

Then she told us she was going to leave the room, and that if the "culprit" returned the dictionary to her desk there wouldn't be any consequences, and there would be no questions asked.

Mrs Craig made Patty Farrell class monitor and left the room. Patty takes her job as class monitor really seriously, and when she's in charge nobody dares to step out of line.

I was just hoping the person who took the dictionary would hurry up and come clean, because I had two cartons of milk for lunch.

MAY I PLEASE USE THE LAVATORY?

NO.

But nobody did come forward. And, sure enough, Mrs Craig stuck to her promise and kept us inside for recess. Then she said she was gonna keep us inside every day until the dictionary was returned.

Friday
Mrs Craig has kept us inside for the past three days, and still no dictionary. Today Patty Farrell was sick, so Mrs Craig put Alex Aruda in charge of the room while she was gone.

Alex is a good student, but people aren't afraid of Alex the way they are of Patty Farrell. As soon as Mrs Craig left the room, it was complete pandemonium.

A couple of guys who were sick of getting stuck inside for recess every day decided to try to figure out who took Mrs Craig's dictionary.

The first person they interrogated was this kid named Corey Lamb. I think Corey was number one on the list of suspects because he's smart and he's always using big words.

Corey fessed up to the crime in no time flat. But it turns out he only said he did it because the pressure made him crack.

The next kid on the list was Peter Lynn, and before you knew it Peter was confessing, too.

I figured it was just a matter of time before those guys cornered ME. So I knew I had to think up something fast.

I've read enough Sherlock Sammy books to know that sometimes it takes a nerd to get you out of a pinch. And I figured if anyone could crack this case it was Alex Aruda.

So me and a couple of other guys who were

worried about getting hassled went over to Alex to see if he could help us out.

We told Alex we needed him to solve the mystery of who took Mrs Craig's dictionary, but he didn't even know what we were TALKING about. I guess Alex had been so wrapped up in his book that he hadn't even noticed what had been going on around him for the past couple of days.

Plus, Alex always stays inside to read during recess, so Mrs Craig's punishment hadn't had a big effect on his life.

Unfortunately, Alex has read his share of Sherlock Sammy books, too, so he said he would help us if we paid him five bucks. Me and the other guys agreed it was worth it, and we pooled our money, then forked over the five dollars.

We laid out all the facts of the case to Alex, but we didn't know a whole lot. Then we asked Alex if he could get us pointed in the right direction.

I expected Alex to start taking notes and spout some scientific mumbo jumbo, but all he did was close the book he was reading and show the cover to us. And you're not gonna BELIEVE this, but it was Mrs Craig's dictionary.

Alex said he'd been studying the dictionary to get ready for the state spelling bee next month. Well, THAT would've been nice to know BEFORE we gave him our five bucks.

Anyway, there was no time to waste complaining, because Mrs Craig was gonna be back in the room at any second.

Corey Lamb grabbed the book from Alex and put it on Mrs Craig's desk. But she walked in the room right at that moment.

Mrs Craig ended up going back on her whole "no consequences" promise, so Corey Lamb is gonna be spending the next three weeks inside during recess.

Looking on the bright side, though, at least he'll have Alex Aruda to keep him company.

Corey is stuck inside at break time. Can you help him colour in the picture to survive the boredom?

The dictionary has gone missing again!
Can you work out who has taken it?

Alex   Greg   Patty   Mrs Craig

Good advice for next year's class

Here are some top
school-survival tips from Greg.

1. Don't use the bathroom on the second floor,
because there aren't any stall doors in there.

2. Be careful who you sit next to in the cafeteria.

3. Don't pick your nose right before you get your school picture taken.

Can you write your own list?

1.

2.

3.

SCHOOL ELECTIONS AND TOILET-PAPER MAYHEM

from

THE THIRD WHEEL

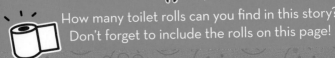

<u>Monday</u>
Everyone was excited to find out who the guest was for today's assembly.

But it turned out there WASN'T a guest. After we sat down in the gym, Vice Principal Roy got up on the stage and said the reason he gathered us all together was to announce that there was gonna be a special election to replace the student council.

We had student council elections in the autumn. But the class officers were skipping the meetings because they're held during recess, and I guess the advisors got fed up.

Vice Principal Roy said there are two conditions for running for office. One, you have to be willing to attend all the student council meetings. And, two, you can't have three detentions or more.

I felt like that second rule was directed at ME, because I just picked up my third detention.

In my first year of middle school, an eighth-grader told me there was a secret elevator that went to the second floor, and that he could sell me a special pass for five bucks.

That sounded like a good deal to ME, so I gave him five dollars for the pass, which looked pretty official.

ELEVATOR PASS

This pass entitles the
holder to unlimited use of
the middle school elevator.

But it turned out the whole thing was a scam and there was no such thing as a secret elevator.

I'd been holding on to that elevator pass ever since. But a few weeks ago I sold it to a kid who's new to our school.

Unfortunately, I wasn't careful enough, and I got busted by Vice Principal Roy, who made me return the money.

He even gave me a detention, which really stunk, because I'd given the kid a deal by selling him the pass at half price.

After the assembly I realized something: Rowley has never had a detention, so he'd be the PERFECT candidate for student council. I told him he should run, but he said he wouldn't know what he'd do if he got elected.

But that's where I come in. I told him if he gets elected I'll make all the tough decisions and all he'll have to do is show up for the meetings and do what I tell him. I think it's a GENIUS idea, because I'll get to be in power but I won't have to miss any recess.

I offered to be his campaign manager so he won't even have to lift a finger to get elected.

So we went to the bulletin board in the front hallway to sign Rowley up.

I told him he should run for one of the juicy spots like President or Vice President, but he wanted to run for "Social Chairperson". I have no idea what a Social Chairperson does, but as long as Rowley gets to vote on the important decisions I'm fine with it.

<u>Wednesday</u>
Yesterday some of the other candidates
were hanging posters up in the hallways
and handing out buttons to get themselves
elected. So we were ALREADY behind.

I knew I was gonna have to dream up
something big to make sure Rowley gets
elected, so here's what I came up with.

When the candidates give their speeches,
the gym will be full of students.

At sports games I've seen on TV, people in the stadium paint their chests to spell out messages.

Last night I got a bunch of Uncle Gary's T-shirts from the garage, turned them inside out and wrote a letter on each one so they spelled out "VOTE ROWLEY JEFFERSON FOR SOCIAL CHAIRPERSON".

It took all night, and I went through about twenty markers, but I knew it was gonna make a big splash at the assembly.

I got to school early today and gave each kid who was willing to wear a shirt a piece of gum.

Help Greg with his campaign. Design and colour in a T-shirt to win votes for Rowley!

But, when we got into the gym, getting the kids to stand in the right order was like trying to herd cats.

The only candidates who got to give speeches were the ones who were running for President.

I was pretty relieved to hear that, because when I had Rowley rehearse his speech for Social Chairperson he was a nervous wreck.

GREETINGS, FELLOW STUDENTS. MY NAME IS ROWLEY JEFFERSON, AND I, UH...

The first candidate to give a speech was a girl named Sydney Greene who is a straight-A student and has never missed a day of school. She said that if she's elected President she'll get better equipment for the music room and will organize a project to put new protective covers on the books in the library.

Next up was Bryan Buttsy. As soon as Vice Principal Roy called Bryan up to the podium, everyone in the gym started making all sorts of obnoxious noises.

I'm sure Bryan said a lot of interesting things during his speech, but you couldn't hear a word with all that racket.

I just hope Bryan doesn't run for President when he's a grown-up because, if he does, his campaign rallies are gonna be RIDICULOUS.

The last candidate to go was a kid named Eugene Ellis. Eugene is the only person running for President who didn't put up posters or hand out lollipops or anything like that, so nobody really took him seriously.

Eugene's campaign speech was only about thirty seconds long. He said that if he's elected President he'll get the school to replace the cheap toilet paper in the bathrooms with the expensive quilted kind.

When Eugene finished his speech, the whole place went berserk. Kids are ALWAYS complaining about the toilet-paper situation because the type the school uses is like sandpaper.

And, from the reaction Eugene got, I don't think Sydney or Bryan has a prayer.

<u>Thursday</u>
Just like I predicted, Eugene Ellis won
student council President by a landslide.
Rowley won, too, because he was the only
person who actually signed up for Social
Chairperson. I wish I'd known that,
because I could've saved myself a lot of
hassle with those T-shirts.

The student council had their first
meeting today, and Mrs Birch, the
teacher who works with the council,
told Eugene the school couldn't afford
to stock the bathrooms with quilted
toilet paper, so he might as well forget
about it.

Word got around school fast, and people were pretty mad. The whole reason everyone voted for Eugene was because of his campaign promise. Plus, we do fundraisers for the school every year, and you would think they could take some of the money we make and spend it on some quality toilet paper.

Thursday
There have been some pretty big developments at school this week.
It all started on Monday at the last

student council meeting. The meetings are held in the teachers' lounge, and after the Treasurer, Javan Hill, went to use the bathroom he came out with a roll of Pillow-Soft Ultra toilet paper.

That means the teachers have been treating themselves to good toilet paper while us kids are stuck with the cheap stuff.

When Eugene Ellis confronted Mrs Birch, she knew the teachers were totally busted.

Mrs Birch said that even though the teachers use Pillow-Soft Ultra there's not enough money in the budget to stock all the kids' bathrooms with expensive toilet paper, but she could agree to a compromise.

She said the school could allow kids to bring in their OWN rolls from home.

And, when the announcement came over the loudspeaker, it was a huge victory for Eugene Ellis and the rest of the student council.

Tuesday was the first day kids were allowed to bring in their own toilet paper, and I think some people went a little overboard.

In fact, some kids brought in so much toilet paper that there wasn't enough room to fit it in their lockers, so they carried their supply around with them.

Everything probably would've been just fine, but at lunch someone threw a roll of toilet paper at somebody else, and within about fifteen seconds it was a total madhouse.

Later that afternoon the principal got on the loudspeaker and said that from now on we're only allowed to bring five squares of toilet paper to school a day.

That seems like a pretty ridiculous rule, because I don't know ANYONE who can get by on five squares.

Yesterday a few kids got caught bringing in more than they were supposed to, so now the teachers are checking our bags when we come in through the front doors in the morning.

Thursday

By the time the principal set that five-square limit last week, I'd already stocked my locker with about twenty rolls.

The teachers do random checks on kids' lockers now, and I knew sooner or later they were gonna find my secret stash.

I wanted to make sure my supply lasted to the end of the school year, so I needed to figure out how to protect it.

I decided the only way to do THAT was to have a stall in the bathroom all to myself, and to keep my toilet paper hidden in there.

So on Monday I picked a stall that was pretty clean and locked the door. Then I crawled underneath it to get out.

Next I slipped some old trainers I'd brought from home on the floor in front of the toilet to make it look like the stall was occupied.

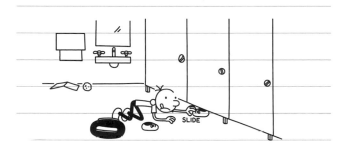

SLIDE

Every time I needed to use the bathroom this week, I waited to make sure no one was around, then I crawled underneath my stall door. It was like I had a tiny little apartment in there. In fact, I wish I'd thought of this idea a long time ago.

For a few days my system worked great. No one even TRIED to use my private stall.

But then I forgot to pick one of the spare shoes up off the ground, and I guess that must've looked pretty suspicious from the outside.

It wasn't long before people figured out I was hoarding quality toilet paper, and things fell apart pretty quickly after that.

The SCOOP on your CLASSMATES

Greg couldn't survive school without his classmates. Who are the people who help you get through school every day?

The person you'd trust to keep your school secrets:

_____

The person who would save you a seat in the cafeteria:

_____

The person who's most likely to
blame a fart on someone else:

_____

The person you'd want to do
your homework for you:

_____

The person who is best
at school pranks:

_____

If you were voted student president, what would you change about your school?

_____

_____

_____

_____

_____

_____

_____

You can find out more about the world of

Diary of a Wimpy Kid

at

www.wimpykidclub.co.uk

ANSWERS PAGE

- There are 11 stripes on Mrs Craig's skirt.

- Mrs Craig has taken the dictionary.

- We found 112 toilet rolls. How many did you spot?